more titles in

The Secret Games of Maximus Todd!

Hyper to the Max
Clever Max invents a game to keep his Super Fidgets at bay for the day.

Frantic Friend Countdown
Everyone's got a best friend except him. But when a new kid arrives at the school, Max plays a secret game to make him Max's buddy.

Big Game Jitters
It's the soccer championship and Max's team is playing the school bully's team. As soon as the match starts, Max's gets a case of the Super Fidgets.

Flu Shot Fidgets
Max is at the doctor's office, when he invents a secret game to calm his Super Fidgets.

School Trip Squirmies
Max is on a school bus on his way to an art gallery when he gets a case of the Super Fidgets.

Camping Chaos

by L. M. Nicodemo

illustrated by Graham Ross

Formac Publishing Company Limited
Halifax

Formac Publishing Company Limited recognizes the support of the Province
of Nova Scotia through Film and Creative Industries Nova Scotia. We are
pleased to work in partnership with the Province of Nova Scotia to develop
and promote our creative industries for the benefit of all Nova Scotians. We
acknowledge the support of the Canada Council for the Arts which last year
invested $157 million to bring the arts to Canadians throughout the country.

Cover design: Tyler Cleroux
Cover image: Graham Ross

Library and Archives Canada Cataloguing in Publication

Title: Camping chaos / L.M. Nicodemo ; illustrated by Graham Ross.
Names: Nicodemo, L. M. (Linda M.), author. | Ross, Graham, 1962- illustrator.
Series: Nicodemo, L. M. (Linda M.). Secret games of Maximus Todd.
Description: Series statement: The secret games of Maximus Todd
Identifiers: Canadiana 20200276018 | ISBN 9781459505834 (hardcover) | ISBN
9781459505841 (softcover)
Classification: LCC PS8627.I245 C36 2021 | DDC jC813/.6—dc23

Formac Publishing Company Limited
5502 Atlantic Street
Halifax, Nova Scotia, Canada
B3H 1G4
www.formac.ca

Distributed in the United States by:
Lerner Publishing Group
241 1st Ave N
Minneapolis, MN, USA
55401

Printed and bound in Canada.
Manufactured by Friesens in Altona, MB in January 2021.
Job #272145

Contents

To my dear children, Michael and Elizabeth. You reside in every story.

ACKNOWLEDGEMENTS

Special thanks to Jackson who shared his family's camping adventures, and through his knack for adding numbers, inspired Max's game.

Chapter One

Five A.M. Wake-up Call

"Wake up," a voice whispered in Maximus Todd's ear. "Time to get ready."

"Mom?" Max muttered, rubbing his eyes.

He stretched his arms in a V and yawned, **"HUUH-aaHaa."**

1

It was still dark in his bedroom and he could only just make out the shadowy outline of his bookshelf and dresser.

Mom leaned over and kissed Max on the top of his curly red hair. "Don't forget to brush your teeth."

He squinted at his Laserman alarm clock perched on the

nightstand. Five a.m. glowed alien green.

FIVE O'CLOCK IN THE MORNING!

Max shook his head. *Why did Mom wake me up so early?*

It was summertime. No school. No classes.

Has Mom Lost Her Marbles?

Then it came to him. Suddenly, like how the answer to a riddle could pop into his head out of the blue.

We Leave on Our Camping Trip Today. WOOHOO!

Every summer Max's family towed their trailer to Camp Friendly Pines. This year's vacation was EXTRA-special because his best friend, Shiv Pal, would be joining them.

SPROING.

Max leaped out of bed, flicked on the lights and grabbed the clothes on his chair. *The sooner I'm dressed, the sooner we're going.*

But rushing made Max take twice as long. Only after FOUR tries did he finally get his T-shirt on right.

First time. Backwards.

Second time. Inside out.

Third time. Head stuck in a sleeve.

Shiv's never camped before. We'll have so much fun hiking in the woods and skipping stones at the lake. Max grabbed his ball cap and grinned.

PLUS,

WE WON'T HAVE TO SHOWER FOR DAYS!

The trip was practically perfect except . . .

His grin instantly flipped to a frown. *I wish the Bokelys weren't coming.*

The Bokelys were good friends of Max's mom. He was grateful they could drive Shiv to Friendly Pines. But why did they have to bring along their pesky daughter?

Max squinched his nose. Mandy Beth Bokely. **UGH!** She was the stone in his shoe, the worm in his apple, the pimple on his nose.

Maybe an eagle will fly over our campsite and carry her off.

He snickered. Maybe —

"Maaax," called Mom from downstairs, "We're leaving in ten minutes."

Maybe . . . *I should finish getting ready.*

Chapter Two

Camp Friendly Pines

When Max awoke the second
time that day, Mom was turning
their car onto a gravel road.
Sarah, his baby sister, was
asleep in her car seat beside
him.

He peered through the rear

window. Their trailer followed along like a puppy on a leash.

"Good morning, sleepy head," Max's grandfather said. He held a travel mug in one hand and a map in the other. Granpops didn't trust the GPS.

"Computer glitches," he'd say, "and we'll end up at the North Pole."

"Good morning," said Max.

"ARE WE THERE YET?"

"As a matter of fact, we are," replied Mom as they passed a big wooden sign that read, "Welcome to Camp Friendly Pines. We put the WILD in WILDERNESS!"

Max rolled down his window. Along the road grew tall clumps of trees, and beyond that, rocky hills. The air smelled of pine needles.

At the campground entrance, a park ranger sat by the window of a little brick building. Max's mom pulled their car up. It reminded Max of the drive-thru at Dee-Licious Donuts.

"GOOD MORNING,"
SAID THE RANGER.
"HOW CAN I HELP
YOU FOLKS?"

"I'll have a vanilla donut with rainbow sprinkles, please," Max joked.

The ranger laughed. "Nothing better than a camper with a sense of humour," she said.

Mom smiled. "We have a reservation under the Todd family."

The ranger handed Mom a camping permit and some pamphlets. "Here's a park map and a list of rules."

"RULES?" Max perked up. Anything about banning

annoying eight-year-old pests
named Mandy Beth?

"Safety tips on how to build
a campfire. Rules about not
disturbing the wildlife. But
MOST important of all," the
ranger winked, "what to do if
you run into a bear."

"YOU'VE GOT B-B-BEARS HERE?!?" stuttered Max.

"No, but there's a first time for everything." She chuckled. Then Mom and Granpops laughed too.

WHAT'S SO FUNNY?

thought Max, swallowing the sudden lump in his throat.

Chapter Three

Pitching the Tent

"YOU MADE IT," cried out
Max when the Bokelys pulled
up. "I've been here for-EVER."
To Max, the ten minutes of
waiting for their arrival felt like
an eternity.

Shiv jumped out of the van.

"THiS PLaCe iS SUPeR COOL!"

he said. "The trees are gi-normous. And we counted five deer on our way in!"

"Wait'll you see the rest of the park, Shiv. You'll never

want to leave," Max told his best friend.

"That's right," joined Mandy Beth.

"YOU'RE GOING TO HAVE A BLAST."

"Oh . . . Mandy Beth," Max mumbled. "I forgot you were coming." He glanced up at the sky.

"See something, Max?" Mandy Beth asked.

"UN-fortunately, no," Max said, wishing he'd spied an eagle.

"Hey, do you kids want to help set up the tent?" Granpops called.

Max, Mandy Beth and Shiv jogged over to Granpops, who was unloading a duffle bag from the trunk of the car.

"Okay. Where do you want it?" asked Max's grandfather.

The three surveyed the campsite. Max propped his fist under his chin and thought hard.

Near the bushes? He shook his head. No, they'd get attacked by mosquitoes.

At the edge of the woods? He shook his head again. No way. The maybe-there-are-bears would get them.

"How about over here?"

offered Mandy Beth, pointing
between the two trailers.

Max walked over to the spot.
He paced the area. "Size seems
right," he mumbled.

THEN HE STOMPED UP AND DOWN.

"NO QUICKSAND."

Finally, he licked his finger and held it high in the air. "Wind's blocked too."

Mandy Beth put her hands on her hips. "C'mon, Max."

Max hated to admit it, but she had picked the perfect location. *Ugh! She's such a know-it-all!*

"Well-ll-ll, I guess," Max muttered.

"YES!"

shouted Mandy Beth and Shiv, doing a fist bump.

"Let's get to it then," said Granpops, unfolding the tent instructions.

ONe. TWO. THRee.

In no time they laid the tarp, staked the poles and hitched up the tent.

Now Max was ready to do some real camping.

Chapter Four

Feed Mandy Beth to the Bears

"Get your stuff, and we'll set up inside the tent," Max said to Shiv.

"Hey! What about me?" asked Mandy Beth.

"Wouldn't you rather sleep in the trailer?" said Max. "The ground's rock hard."

Mandy Beth shrugged. "My sleeping bag is extra fluffy."

"And, if a bear attacks, it'll eat you first," added Max. "Even though you probably taste like broccoli soup."

Mandy Beth scowled. "There aren't bears here. Besides, you better be nice to me or I'll tell your mom that you once ate an eraser."

"It looked like chewing gum," huffed Max. "Anyone could have made that mistake."

The boys rolled out their sleeping bags. "Put yours over there," Max told Mandy Beth, pointing at the far wall.

"No way," said Mandy Beth. "I don't want my head near

YOUR STINKY FEET."

"My feet smell like roses," said Max.

"Sure," replied Mandy Beth. "Dried up, mouldy ones."

Shiv made a suggestion. "Lay the sleeping bags like the spokes of a wheel. Our heads go in the middle and our feet at the ends."

"AND NOBODY'S TOES-ES WILL GET in anyone's noses," Max RHYMED.

Next, Max dumped out his backpack.

"Let's go over our rations. That means *food* in camp-talk," he explained, looking at Mandy Beth. She shot an I-already-know-that glare. "I've got granola bars and grapes," he said.

Shiv peered into his backpack. "I brought lemon

cookies that my sister made
and juice boxes."

"Great! Mandy Beth?" said
Max.

Mandy Beth stuck out
her chin. "Um, I didn't bring
anything."

"Geez, Mandy Beth!" Max smacked his hand against his forehead. **"WE NEED FOOD TO SURVIVE."**

Mandy Beth rolled her eyes. "Can't we just unzip the tent flap and go into one of the trailers if we get hungry?"

"Forget it," Max groaned. Clearly, Mandy Beth knew nothing about living in the wild. "What about entertainment? I brought my favourite joke book." Max opened a worn paperback.

"Hey, guys, why don't mummies go on camping trips?"

Shiv shrugged. "I dunno."

"THEY'RE AFRAID TO RELAX AND UNWIND!" GIGGLED MAX.

"I have some *Laserman and the Cyborgs of Justice* comic books," said Shiv.

"And I've got this," said Mandy Beth. She pulled out a book titled *Spooky Campfire Tales*. It had a picture on the front of people around a campfire. The dark outline of a cloud partly covered a full moon.

Max leaned forward.

THAT'S NO CLOUD!

It was a wailing ghost with skeleton hands.

Mandy Beth's eyes grew large as she read from the back of the book: "These chilling stories of ghosts, ghouls and goblins will petrify even the bravest of hearts. Read on . . .

iF YOU DaRe."

"Oooh, that'll be good for late at night," said Shiv.

Max despised ghost stories. He hated feeling afraid, how the hairs went up on the back of his neck, how his hands turned clammy.

"BOR-iNG,"

Max said, his eyelids drooping. He fell back onto his sleeping bag, pretending to nod off. "Keraw-shoo," he snored.

Mandy Beth slugged him with her pillow. "You're scared," she said.

"KeRawww-SHOOOO," Max snored louder. It was easy to drown her out.

Chapter Five

Call of the Wild

Having arranged their camping gear, Max, Mandy Beth and Shiv popped out from the tent.

"We're going on a hike,"

announced Max. "Who wants to come?"

"Count us in," said Max's mother as she put Sarah in a carrier on her back.

"Me too," said Ms. Bokely. "I want to work up a good appetite, so I can indulge in a few s'mores tonight."

"WHAT ARE S'MORES?"
ASKED SHIV.

"You REALLY don't know much about camping," said Max, feeling instantly sorry for his best friend.

"It's a cookie," piped up Mandy Beth, "made of ooey, gooey marshmallow —"

"And melted chocolate," said Max, licking his lips.

"Between two graham crackers," sighed Ms. Bokely. "They're my greatest weakness."

"Wow," laughed Shiv. "I can't wait to try them."

The hikers headed along a narrow path that cut through

the forest. For a while, no one spoke. Woodland sounds of rustling and chirping filled the air.

Max stooped and picked up a long branch. "Real campers have walking sticks," he said, handing it to Shiv. "You can lean on it, test how deep water is and use it to move stuff out of the way."

PLUS, iT MiGHT BE HaNDY iF WE RUN iNTO a BEaR.

"Good idea," said Mom. "Can you find one for Mandy Beth too?"

"Could you, Max?" asked Mandy Beth in a fake-sugary voice.

Max grimaced.

i'm Gonna Puke!

But with Mom and Ms. Bokely tagging along, he had no choice.

He reached under a nearby
bush to grab an old branch.
"OWWW!" he cried out, yanking
back his hand.
"OW-OW-OW!"
Max held up his finger. At
the side bloomed an angry red
splotch.

"Oh dear!" said Mom. "You've been stung."

Max's eyes watered. His finger felt itchy and hot. He shook his hand, but the sharp pain would not go away.

"That's gotta hurt," said Shiv, patting Max on the back.

Mom gently took hold of Max's hand. "No stinger. Still, we better head back and get some ice on it."

Max gulped. "I'm fine. Let's keep going."

"Your mom's right, Max," said Ms. Bokely. "Besides, look at the sky."

Dark storm clouds were

rolling in. Lightning glimmered in the distance. The group turned around and hurried down the path. Max held his hand against his chest, but with every step his finger throbbed.

Real campers get stung all the time, he thought, trying to be brave. *Living in the wilderness, stuff happens.*

STORMS . . . BEES . . . BEARS . . . GHOSTS WITH SKELETON HANDS.

Suddenly the clouds busted overhead. A downpour. Without

warning Max's brain fuzzled
and his mouth fizzled and in his
ears echoed a whoosh-whoosh
sound.

OH NO, HE THOUGHT, MY SUPER FIDGETS!

Chapter Six

Fidgets in the Forest

Once in a while, usually at the **WORST** of times, Max's Super Fidgets attacked. Overloaded with too much energy, Max couldn't listen, couldn't sit still, couldn't focus.

He felt his arms grow

FLiPPY FLOPPY.

His legs, **WiBBLY WOBBLY.**
He hopped up and down and
swung his elbows out like a
chicken.

Max couldn't help it.

"Hey, do you need to go to the bathroom?" Mandy Beth asked him, crinkling her nose.

Max glared. What he needed was a game. Only by making up a secret game that kept his mind busy on the inside could he stay calm on the outside.

THINK! THINK! THINK!

He recalled setting up the tent and planning the hike. Mom had said "Count us in." Then they'd told Shiv about s'mores —

Count? S'mores? Aha! I know.

I'LL ADD UP NUMBERS TO FEND OFF THE FIDGETS!

Then Max grudgingly set the stakes. And *if I stop adding . . . if I lose my game,* **I'LL . . . I'LL GIVE UP TONIGHT'S S'MORES.**

The dark sky flashed. A blast rumbled through the treetops. The trail quickly turned to mud.

"Run ahead, you three," Ms. Bokely told Max, Mandy Beth and Shiv. "You're about five minutes from the campsite if you hustle."

My game begins! Max smirked. *Three! Five! . . . Um, three plus five equals eight.* A calm settled in. Max kicked a skip and ran after his friends through the pouring rain.

Chapter Seven

Stinky Feet

Outside the trailer, Granpops
held an umbrella overhead
while Mr. Bokely tended to
Max's sting.

**"THE BEST CURE FOR A SORE
FINGER IS TO CUT IT OFF,"**
he told Max.

"My opinion exactly," added Max's grandfather.

Max's eyes popped. "Too bad I forgot to bring my chainsaw." Mr. Bokely frowned. "I guess I'll just spray it with disinfectant. This might hurt a little."

"That's okay," Max said, relieved.

"Keep the ice on for about ten minutes, and you should be good," Mr. Bokely advised.

TEN, NOTICED MAX. EIGHT PLUS TEN EQUALS EIGHTEEN.

Pressing the cold pack on his newly bandaged finger, Max followed his friends into their dry tent. They hung their wet jackets on pole pegs and then peeled off their soggy shoes and socks.

"PEEE-U!"

cried Shiv. "My wet socks smell like rotten onions."

"Mine smell like burnt Brussels sprouts," Mandy Beth

snorted. "What about yours,
Max?"

Max lifted his dripping socks
with his good hand and sniffed.

"Mmmm. Roses."

Mandy Beth's eyebrows shot up. "Liar!"

"See for yourself," he said, hurling them at her. One slid off her chin. The other stuck to her forehead.

"EWWW!"

Mandy Beth shrieked and quickly flung Max's socks at Shiv.

Shiv caught them and pushed the socks to his nose. "Yep." He nodded. "Roses." Then he rolled his eyes and pretended to faint.

Laughing, the three friends settled atop their sleeping bags.

"Let's play Tipping Tower,"
said Mandy Beth.

"We can have a couple
of my cookies," added Shiv,
pulling the container from his
backpack.

A couple means two, Max
realized. *Two plus eighteen is*

twenty. "My finger's still sore. I don't think I can keep my hand steady enough."

"You probably can't hold the cards for Crazy Eights either," said Shiv.

Max counted in his head. *Eight.*

EIGHT PLUS TWENTY EQUALS TWENTY-EIGHT.

"I know!" Mandy Beth clapped her hands. "I'll read you a spooky story from my book."

"Okay," Shiv remarked. "It'll be like watching a scary movie without the pictures."

Max didn't know what to say.
A ghost tale for sure would
set his knees knocking and his
stomach somersaulting.

BRMM-DRMM!

Thunder rumbled outside.

"The townsfolk claim that
the old Finster house on Crest
Hill is haunted by a ghost."
Mandy Beth read in a low, eerie
voice. Shiv munched quietly
on a cookie. Max squeezed his
eyes shut, hoping he wouldn't
have nightmares. "But the truth

is there isn't just one spectre."

One, thought Max. *One plus twenty-eight is twenty-nine.*

"A family of four sinister spirits float through its abandoned hallways."

Four plus twenty-nine equals thirty-three, Max added in his head. A cold shiver crawled up his spine.

"This is the true and terrifying tale of how three teenagers decide to spend a night in that ramshackle house and prove there are no such things as ghosts."

Another number. Three and thirty-three make thirty-six.

Max grunted. **"WHY WOULD anyone stay overnight in a haunted house?** What a dumb thing to do."

"Yeah," agreed Shiv. "I've got goosebumps just thinking about it."

"Pwock, pwock," clucked Mandy Beth. "It's only a story, guys."

As she continued, Max concentrated in case a number popped up. Strangely, he forgot about his sore finger and about being scared. By "The End," Max had counted up to forty-two, and the sun had returned.

Chapter Eight

Scavenger Hunt

Shiv unzipped the tent flap.
Max squinted his eyes. Not a
single cloud in the gumball-blue
sky.

"Welcome back to nature,"
Ms. Bokely said, handing a
sheet of paper to Mandy Beth.

"We made you a scavenger hunt while hunkered down in the trailer."

Max scanned through the list. Acorns. *Easy peasy.* But a bullfrog? *Not so much.*

"See how many you can locate before supper," said Max's mom. "You've got about thirty minutes."

Max's ears pricked. *Thirty. Thirty plus forty-two equals seventy-two.*

"TO THE LAKE,"
CALLED MANDY BETH.

She ran, raising the paper high like she was leading a parade.

Max and Shiv chased after her.

They arrived at the lake out of breath. A light breeze pushed the tall grasses and cattails at the water's edge so they looked as if they waved to Max and his friends. Other campers were fishing from the dock.

"What's the first item?" asked Shiv.

"Three pinecones," said Mandy Beth.

Max narrowed his eyebrows.
THREE PLUS SEVENTY-TWO IS SEVENTY-FIVE.
"But," she continued, "It'd be better to look over the whole list. We might come across some things while searching for others."

"Good idea," said Shiv.

Max panicked. "Bad idea," he said. He'd seen the items.

LOTS OF THINGS TO FIND AND LOTS OF NUMBERS TOO!

"It'll be confusing."

Mandy Beth kicked at the dirt. "Don't pay attention then, Max . . . Um, three pinecones, a fishing lure, two things that are orange, four different kinds of leaves, five stones smaller than a big toe —"

"Ha ha," laughed Shiv. "Since your feet smell like roses, Max, we'll use your toe to measure."

Max didn't hear. He was too
busy calculating. *Three and
seventy-five is seventy-eight
. . . plus two . . . or was it four?*
Oh no! Max already lost track.

"AaHHH!" Max moaned,

laying his head in his hands.
The tops of his ears burned
bright red. **"STOP! STOP!"**

Shiv nudged his elbow.
"What's wrong, buddy?"

Mandy Beth and Shiv were
the only people in the whole
world who knew about Max's
Super Fidgets. "I'm having an
EPISODE," he confessed.

"Super Fidgets?" Mandy Beth
asked. Max squeezed his eyes
to stop the tears and gave a
little nod. "But, Max, why didn't
you say something?"

He shrugged. "I didn't want
to wreck Shiv's first camp-out."

"WHAT?

i'm having the best time!"

Shiv grinned. "No way a few
Super Fidgets could change
that."

"Tell us your game," Mandy
Beth urged. "Maybe we can
help."

Max wiped his face with his
sleeve. "Okay. But I still want
to do the scavenger hunt."

Mandy Beth glanced at her
watch. "No probs. Twenty
minutes left."

"Ah-hah," half-chuckled Max.
**"PL-eeease. NO MORE
numbers . . ."**

Chapter Nine

Granpops's
Buns

Granpops waved Max, Shiv and Mandy Beth over when they got back from the lake.

"I have to send you all on a top secret mission," he said. "We need hotdog buns. I forgot to pack them."

Only one place at Friendly Pines sold groceries. "Woohoo! The general store!" cried Max. He swung an arm around Shiv's neck. "Wait till you see all the cool camping gear. Compasses and binoculars and —"

"Oh, you won't have time to look around. Fifteen minutes tops, before supper," said Granpops, handing Max money.

After the hunt, Max had left off at one hundred twenty-eight. A much bigger total than he ever imagined. *Fifteen plus one hundred twenty-eight . . . ooh, that has a carry . . . um . . . one hundred forty-three.*

"One hundred forty-three," Max muttered. His friends gave a thumbs-up.

His game was easier now that shiv and mandy Beth Helped.

Granpops wasn't done. "Wait! Will one package be enough?"

One plus one hundred forty-three equals one hundred forty-four.

Max's grandfather scratched his head. "There are **eight** buns in a package. And there are **seven** of us. Sarah doesn't count because she's only **TWO**

and can't have hotdogs . . ."

Max flinched. Seemed every
second word Granpops spouted
was a number! *Eight and one
hundred forty-four is . . . one
hundred fifty-two. Plus seven*

makes *one hundred fifty-
nine. Add two more . . .* He
caught Mandy Beth tilting her
head and silently moving her
lips. She was adding too. Shiv
counted on his fingers.

"Better buy two packages,
Max," his grandfather said.

"Will do, Granpops!"

i'm at one hundred sixty-one, i think . . .

*Two and one hundred sixty-one
is one hundred sixty-three.*

"Yep," muttered Granpops,
his eyes looking up at the sky.
"That'll give us sixteen buns in
total. More than enough."

"'Kay, Granpops." Sixteen and one hundred sixty-three equals one hundred eighty-nine . . . no . . . one hundred seventy-nine. Max raked his

fingers through his hair. His brain hurt.

Mandy Beth grabbed Max's sleeve. "We gotta get out of here before your grandfather starts counting the corncobs."

"Or the leaves in the salad," Shiv joked.

"HOLD ON THERE!"

Granpops ordered. "You're going to need more money." He pulled out his wallet. "Hand over the five I gave you and take this ten."

Geesh! That's fifteen. And

fifteen plus one hundred seventy-nine is . . . is . . .

Max felt like a human calculator. One with jammed buttons and a low battery.

"Don't forget to thank the clerk," Granpops shouted as Max, Mandy Beth and Shiv raced to the store.

"One hundred ninety-four!" Max shouted back.

Chapter Ten

Win Some Lose Some

Stars poked through the night sky as everyone gathered around the campfire after dinner. Mr. Bokely passed out plates.

"WOOHOO!" Max, Shiv and Mandy Beth cheered.

S'MORE TIME!

Max wiggled marshmallows onto the barbecue forks. Mandy Beth broke chocolate squares and laid them on graham crackers. Now they were ready to teach Shiv.

"Pay attention," Max told his friend. "Don't put the marshmallow right in the flames or it'll burn up."

Mandy Beth slowly spun her fork. "I like to toast mine evenly on all sides."

Max held his marshmallow near the glowing embers and sighed. **A PERFECT DAY.**

Despite the bee sting AND the bears AND the ghosts AND his Super Fidgets.

"Hey, look at that star," he said, pointing up. "It's brighter than any of the others."

"Make a wish, Max," Shiv said.

Max closed his eyes.

"i wish we can camp all summer."

When he opened them, he noticed the golden brown of his marshmallow. "Mine's ready!" Max pulled it from his fork, laid it on the chocolate and topped it with a cracker. Brown and white goo squeezed out the sides.

MMMMMM.

He raised the s'more to his watering mouth.

"Actually, that's not a star. It's the planet Venus," Mandy Beth's mother suddenly spoke.

"Fun fact: Venus is forty million kilometres away. Pretty close. Though not as near as the moon. That's only three hundred eighty-four thousand four hundred kilometres from here."

MAX'S HAND FROZE.

The s'more hovered so
close he could smell it. *Did Ms.
Bokely just say some numbers?*

HOPELESSLY GIGANTIC
NUMBERS?
IMPOSSIBLE-TO-ADD KIND OF
NUMBERS?

"Oh! And another fun fact,"
Ms. Bokely continued. "The sun
is one hundred fifty-one million
kilometres from earth."

Fun facts? More like make-
Max-FAIL facts! Warm chocolate

dripped onto Max's thumb as
he unhappily placed the s'more
down on his plate. No way
could he total those super-
sized numbers! Even with help
from his friends.

LOST.
He LOST His Game!

At the very end. After all the
adding. All the carrying over.
The gazillion numbers he'd had
to juggle.

Darn my stupid fidgets. Max
hung his head.

Shiv threw an arm around

Max's shoulders. "Tomorrow's another day, buddy. You'll —"

"WATCH OUT!"

Mandy Beth shrieked, waving wildly at Shiv's fork and accidentally spilling her plate. Max looked up in time to see

his friend's marshmallow blaze
up, blacken and fall onto the
crackling logs.

"Oh no!" Mandy Beth moaned
as she picked up her s'more.
Bits of dirt and flecks of dried
leaves stuck to the melted
chocolate.

"LOOKS LiKE WE'RE aLL iN THE SAME BOAT."

Shiv shrugged. Then all at
once, the three friends started
laughing.

"Actually." Max smiled,
offering his plate. "You guys
can split mine."

"You ought to make another

wish, Max," piped in Ms. Bokely,
". . . for some more s'mores."
She passed over the fixings.
"Yep. Two hundred fifty billion
stars to choose from . . .
though you know, no one's ever
exactly counted."